MARVEL SUPER HERO ADVENTURES: TO WAKANDA AND BEYOND. Contains material originally published in magazine form as MARVEL SUPER HERO ADVENTURES: SPIDER-MAN AND THE STOLEN VIBRANIUM #1; THE SPIDER-DOCTOR #1; WEBS AND ARROWS AND ANTS, OH MY! #1; MS. MARVEL AND THE TELEPORTING DOG #1; and INFERNO #1. Third printing 2019. ISBN 978-1-302-91230-7. Published by MARVEL WORLDWIDE, INC., a subsidiary of MARVEL ENTERTAINMENT, LLC. OFFICE OF PUBLICATION: 135 West 50th Street, New York, NY 10020. © 2018 MARVEL No similarity between any of the names, characters, persons, and/or institutions in this magazine with those of any living or dead person or institution is intended, and any such similarity which may exist is purely coincidental. **Printed in Canada.** DAN BUCKLEY, President, Marvel Entertainment; JOHN NEE, Publisher; JOE QUESADA, Chief Creative Officer; TOM BREVOORT, SVP of Publishing; DAVID BOGART, Associate Publisher & SVP of Talent Affairs; Publishing & Partnership; DAVID GABRIEL, VP of Print & Digital Publishing; JEFF YOUNGQUIST, VP of Production & Special Projects; DAN CARR, Executive Director of Publishing Technology; ALEX MORALES, Director of Publishing Operations; DAN EDINGTON, Managing Editor; SUSAN CRESPI, Production Manager; STAN LEE, Chairman Emeritus. For information regarding advertising in Marvel Comics or on Marvel.com, please contact Vit DeBellis, Custom Solutions & Integrated Advertising Manager, at vdebellis@marvel.com. For Marvel subscription inquiries, please call 888-511-5480. **Manufactured between 9/25/2019 and 10/15/2019 by SOLISCO PRINTERS, SCOTT, QC, CANADA.**

10 9 8 7 6 5 4 3

TO WAKANDA AND BEYOND

Jim McCann
writer

Dario Brizuela
artist

Dario Brizuela & **Chris Sotomayor**
color artists

VC's Joe Caramagna
letterer

Gurihiru & **Jacob Chabot**
cover art

Sarah Brunstad
editor

Sana Amanat
consulting editor

special thanks to
Derek Laufman

collection editor Jennifer Grünwald
assistant editor Caitlin O'Connell
associate managing editor Kateri Woody
editor, special projects Mark D. Beazley
vp production & special projects Jeff Youngquist
svp print, sales & marketing David Gabriel

book designers Adam Del Re

editor in chief C.B. Cebulski
chief creative officer Joe Quesada
president Dan Buckley
executive producer Alan Fine

Spider-Man and the Stolen Vibranium

cover by Gurihiru

Move it, lady!

Maybe *you* should be the one to move.

BUMP

Upsy-daisy, before you *hurt* someone.

THWIP

Wha?!

Luckily, your friendly neighborhood *Spider-Man* was here to stop you!

Especially since you've got all those *stolen diamonds* in your pockets.

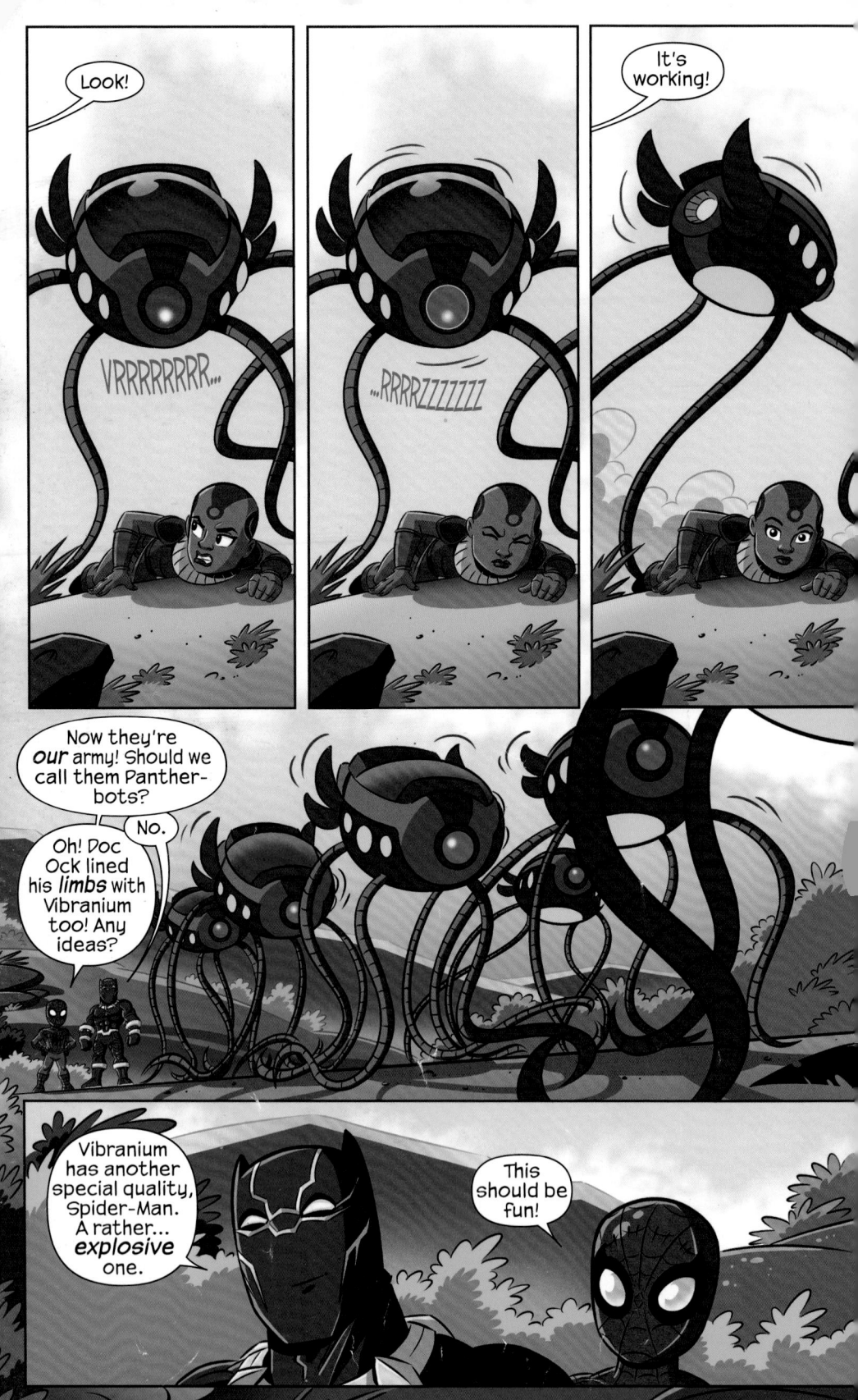

Marvel Super Hero Adventures: Spider-Man and the Stolen Vibranium variant cover by
Khary Randolph & **Emilio Lopez**

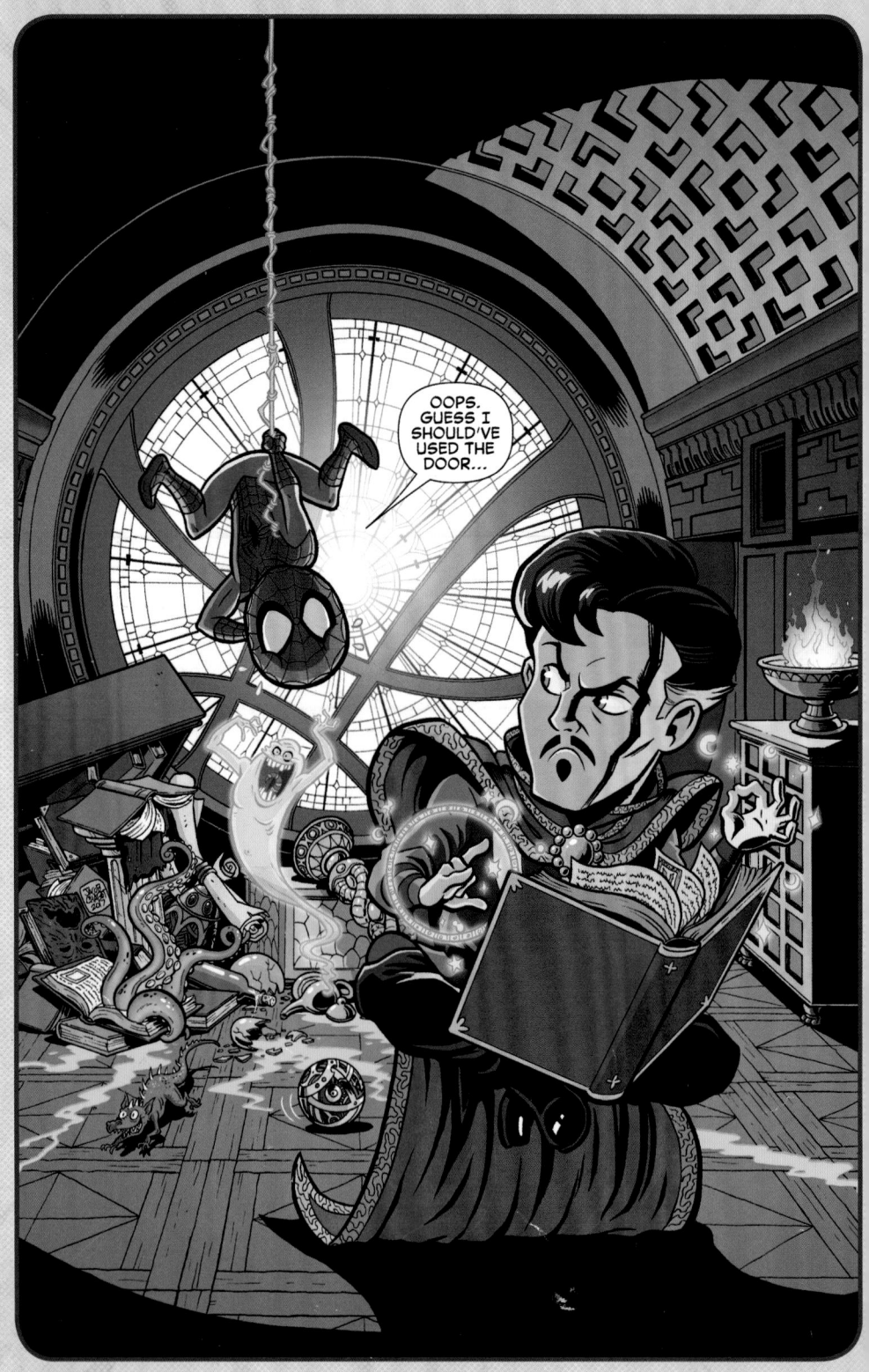

The Spider-Doctor
cover by Jacob Chabot

Webs and Arrows and Ants, Oh My!

cover by Jacob Chabot

That's me, "Webs."

But where's the **other** Hawkeye, **Clint Barton?**

I called Kate first. She's my friend--I knew she'd come help me out!

I was the **second** call?

Look, Clint **trained** me. That's why I took the name "Hawkeye." I **know** what I'm doing here.

All right then, **Hawkeye,** do you know how to get in through the roof?

The **roof?** I have a way better plan...

...*diamond-tip arrow.* Totally cuts through glass.

Usually I prefer things that go boom, but who can say no to diamonds?!

I still think the roof was a good idea...

Can we argue later, like **after** we do some super-heroing?

A *smoke bomb!*

Close your ~cough~ eyes!

SMASH!

HSSSSSSSS

Well, that went worse than expected. Cassie, are you okay?

You should probably rest while we handle Taskmaster... somehow.

I think so...

He has a *photographic memory* that lets his body mimic your every move.

So it's like fighting yourself?

Exactly. So we have to surprise him. Mix it up a little.

Okay, so what tricks do you have?

Hmm. Well, *archery* was clearly a flop...

...And so was shooting *spider-goo.*

Got any more *bright ideas?*

Try and *out-acrobat* him?

You kids... ≥cough≤ So close.

That's my dad's voice! He must be in the next room!

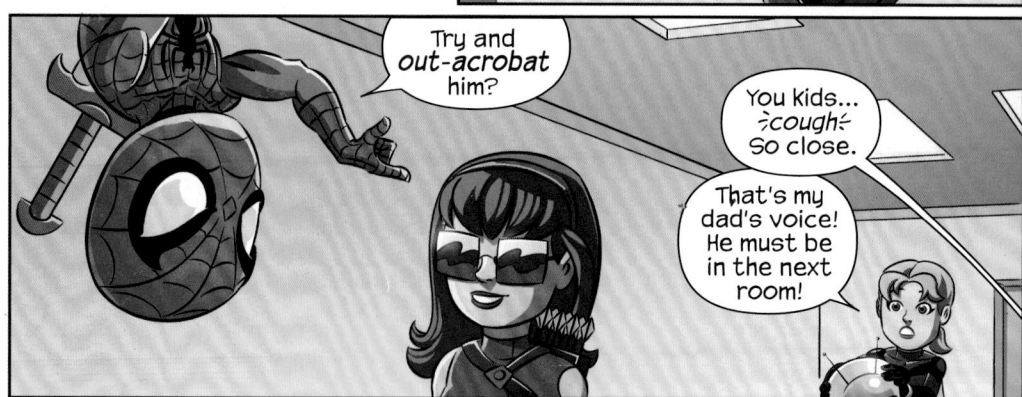

Cass! Are you all right?

Hi, Dad! Taskmaster whammied me with his dis--

Disrupter, I know. Better keep the helmets off for now.

Ant-Man!

Good to see you, Kate. What took you guys so long?

Ms. Marvel and the Teleporting Dog
cover by Jacob Chabot

A FEW MONTHS AGO...
"...it's *never* too late to stand up for yourself. I learned that from a friend I made recently..."
What a beautiful night to web-sling!

Let's see what you have for me across the river.
Sometimes *New Jersey* needs a friendly neighborhood Spider-Man, too.

Psss psss

FWAUM

Garden Snake! Where are you? We must finish the mission!

Yesssss.

Let'sssss finish thissssss...

Wha--

..."Bossssss."

Bah! You're just like the other *heroes* now!

THWIP!

See, Misty? It's never too late to decide who you are and who you really want to be friends with.
Yeah. It's hard being the new girl, but I think I'd like to be more like Abby.
I'm glad. And for what it's worth, you don't have to worry about *ghosts.* This place is--
Gah! Wha? Yeek!
Just *full* of wannabe pranksters... and *spiders*.
Irony.
END

Inferno
cover by Jacob Chabot

Venom. Living alien suit. Bonded to criminal Eddie Brock. Neither one likes Spider-Man.

That's the idea: beat Venom.

The thing is...I'm scared to go full-out *"fwooom,"* you know?

THUMP!

What do you mean? What's wrong?

Well, sometimes when I use my powers like that, it can get *out of control.*

Oooh! That's okay. We'll work through it together!

I'll hit him from above, then *you* hit him with your *fire.*

O...okay. I guess.

MARVEL RISING

THE MARVEL UNIVERSE IS A RICH TREASURE CHEST OF CHARACTERS BORN ACROSS MARVEL'S INCREDIBLE 80-YEAR HISTORY. FROM CAPTAIN AMERICA TO CAPTAIN MARVEL, IRON MAN TO IRONHEART, THIS IS AN EVER-EXPANDING UNIVERSE FULL OF POWERFUL HEROES THAT ALSO REFLECTS THE WORLD WE LIVE IN.

YET DESPITE THAT EXPANSION, OUR STORIES REMAIN TIMELESS. THEY'VE BEEN SHARED ACROSS THE GLOBE AND ACROSS GENERATIONS, LINKING FANS WITH THE ENDURING IDEA THAT ORDINARY PEOPLE CAN DO EXTRAORDINARY THINGS. IT'S THAT SHARED EXPERIENCE OF THE MARVEL STORY THAT HAS ALLOWED US TO EXIST FOR THIS LONG. WHETHER YOUR FIRST MARVEL EXPERIENCE WAS THROUGH A COMIC BOOK, A BEDTIME STORY, A MOVIE OR A CARTOON, WE BELIEVE OUR STORIES STAY WITH AUDIENCES THROUGHOUT THEIR LIVES.

MARVEL RISING IS A CELEBRATION OF THIS TIMELESSNESS. AS OUR STORIES PASS FROM ONE GENERATION TO THE NEXT, SO DOES THE LOVE FOR OUR HEROES. FROM THE CLASSIC TO THE NEWLY IMAGINED, THE PASSION FOR ALL OF THEM IS THE SAME. IF YOU'VE BEEN READING COMICS OVER THE LAST FEW YEARS, YOU'LL KNOW CHARACTERS LIKE MS. MARVEL, SQUIRREL GIRL, AMERICA CHAVEZ, SPIDER-GWEN AND MORE HAVE ASSEMBLED A BEVY OF NEW FANS WHILE CAPTIVATING OUR PERENNIAL FANS. EACH OF THESE HEROES IS UNIQUE AND DISTINCT--JUST LIKE THE READERS THEY'VE BROUGHT IN--AND THEY REMIND US THAT NO MATTER WHAT YOU LOOK LIKE, YOU HAVE THE CAPABILITY TO BE POWERFUL, TOO. WE ARE TAKING THE HEROES FROM MARVEL RISING TO NEW HEIGHTS IN AN ANIMATED FEATURE LATER IN 2018, AS WELL AS A FULL PROGRAM OF CONTENT SWEEPING ACROSS THE COMPANY. BUT FIRST WE'RE GOING BACK TO OUR ROOTS AND TELLING A MARVEL RISING STORY IN COMICS: THE FIRST PLACE YOU MET THESE LOVABLE HEROES.

SO IN THE TRADITION OF EXPANDING THE MARVEL UNIVERSE, WE'RE EXCITED TO INTRODUCE MARVEL RISING--THE NEXT GENERATION OF MARVEL HEROES FOR THE NEXT GENERATION OF MARVEL FANS!

SANA AMANAT
VP, CONTENT & CHARACTER DEVELOPMENT

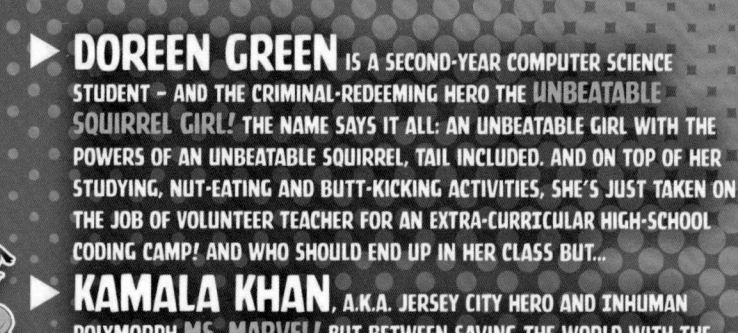

▶ **DOREEN GREEN** IS A SECOND-YEAR COMPUTER SCIENCE STUDENT — AND THE CRIMINAL-REDEEMING HERO THE UNBEATABLE SQUIRREL GIRL! THE NAME SAYS IT ALL: AN UNBEATABLE GIRL WITH THE POWERS OF AN UNBEATABLE SQUIRREL, TAIL INCLUDED. AND ON TOP OF HER STUDYING, NUT-EATING AND BUTT-KICKING ACTIVITIES, SHE'S JUST TAKEN ON THE JOB OF VOLUNTEER TEACHER FOR AN EXTRA-CURRICULAR HIGH-SCHOOL CODING CAMP! AND WHO SHOULD END UP IN HER CLASS BUT...

▶ **KAMALA KHAN,** A.K.A. JERSEY CITY HERO AND INHUMAN POLYMORPH MS. MARVEL! BUT BETWEEN SAVING THE WORLD WITH THE CHAMPIONS AND PROTECTING JERSEY CITY ON HER OWN, KAMALA'S GOT A LOT ON HER PLATE ALREADY. AND FIELD TRIP DAY MAY NOT BE THE BREAK SHE'S ANTICIPATING...

MARVEL RISING
PART 0

DEVIN GRAYSON
WRITER

MARCO FAILLA
ARTIST

RACHELLE ROSENBERG
COLOR ARTIST

VC's CLAYTON COWLES
LETTERER

HELEN CHEN
COVER

JAY BOWEN
DESIGN

HEATHER ANTOS AND **SARAH BRUNSTAD**
EDITORS

SANA AMANAT
CONSULTING EDITOR

C.B. CEBULSKI
EDITOR IN CHIEF

JOE QUESADA
CHIEF CREATIVE OFFICER

DAN BUCKLEY
PRESIDENT

ALAN FINE
EXECUTIVE PRODUCER

SPECIAL THANKS TO RYAN NORTH AND G. WILLOW WILSON

TO BE CONTINUED IN MARVEL RISING!

An Early Chapter Book

MARVEL

SUPER HERO
ADVENTURES

Sand Trap!

By MacKenzie Cadenhead & Sean Ryan

Chapter 1

Peter Parker did not hear his Aunt May talking. He had been pouring the last of the milk into his cereal bowl when the morning news caught his attention.

". . . commotion at the City Bank on Ninety-sixth Street and Columbus Avenue. Police cars are at the scene."

"Peter," Aunt May said again. She shook his shoulder. "Did you hear a word I just said?"

"Sorry, Aunt May," Peter replied.

He looked away from the TV. Aunt May's arms were crossed. *Uh-oh.*

Aunt May was the kindest person Peter knew. She had raised him since he was a little boy. She loved him as much as any parent could. Aunt May was friendly to everyone. And she always threw the ball back when the neighborhood kids lost it over her fence. When Aunt May wasn't smiling, something was wrong.

"Sorry for what?" she asked. "For paying more attention to the television than to your dearest aunt? Or for finishing the milk I asked you to save for my tea party?"

Peter looked at the Cheerios floating in the milk. "Oops," he said. "I forgot."

"Did you also forget that our neighbor Anna is bringing her niece over for tea later?" she asked. "Honestly, Peter. I think you might forget your own name if I didn't call it all the time."

It was true that Peter Parker often forgot to do the things his aunt asked. But it was not for the reason she thought. You see, Peter Parker had a lot on his mind. Peter Parker had a secret.

Peter Parker was Spider-Man!

And sometimes being Spider-Man made being Peter tough.

He looked at his frowning aunt.

I will not be Spider-Man today, he thought. Today I am just Peter Parker. I will be the perfect host for Aunt May's tea party. I will cut the lawn. I will clean my room. I will not get distracted. And I will *not* disappear.

Peter opened his mouth to say all this—except the part about being Spider-Man. But before he could speak, the TV news anchor said something he could not ignore.

"There appears to be a man made of sand leaving the bank with bags full of money. And what do I see? Just like sand through your fingers, this Sandman has slipped past the police! He's headed for Central Park with patrol cars in pursuit! Can anyone stop this powdery plunderer? Or will we bury our heads in the sand as he gets away?"

Chapter 2

"I'll be back with the milk before you know it," Peter said. He stepped onto the sidewalk outside their house in Queens, New York.

"Just to the store, Peter," Aunt May warned from the front door. "Please try not to be late for our guests."

Peter gave his aunt a thumbs-up. He turned the corner and was gone.

It was a bright spring afternoon. Perfect weather for going to the grocery store. Or . . . for sailing through the air on a spiderweb!

"Woo-hoo!" Spider-Man yelled as he swung between skyscrapers. "The Sandman was last seen headed toward Central Park. I bet I can make it there in a New York minute!"

Spider-Man raced into Manhattan. He knew he must catch the Sandman quickly if he wanted to make his tea time.

There was no question that Peter wanted to help Aunt May. He *wanted* to get the milk—he could swing by the grocery store on his way home. He even *wanted* to go to the tea party—everyone

likes a nice cup of Earl Grey, right? But after he was bitten by a radioactive spider and woke up with super powers, Peter had learned that sometimes the tea parties had to wait.

So it was for the webbed warrior. Spider-Man's super heroics were always in demand. Still, having a secret Super Hero identity was not always easy. He could hardly tell his teachers that the Green Goblin ate his homework.

But whenever Peter wondered if

he should hang up his webs and leave crime fighting to the Avengers, the words of his late Uncle Ben helped him make the right choice. "With great power comes great responsibility," Uncle Ben had told him.

No matter what was happening in Peter Parker's world, Spider-Man would always answer a call for help!